The Shoe Type of Women Journal

By: Whitley Witcher

SHOE TYPE OF WOMEN

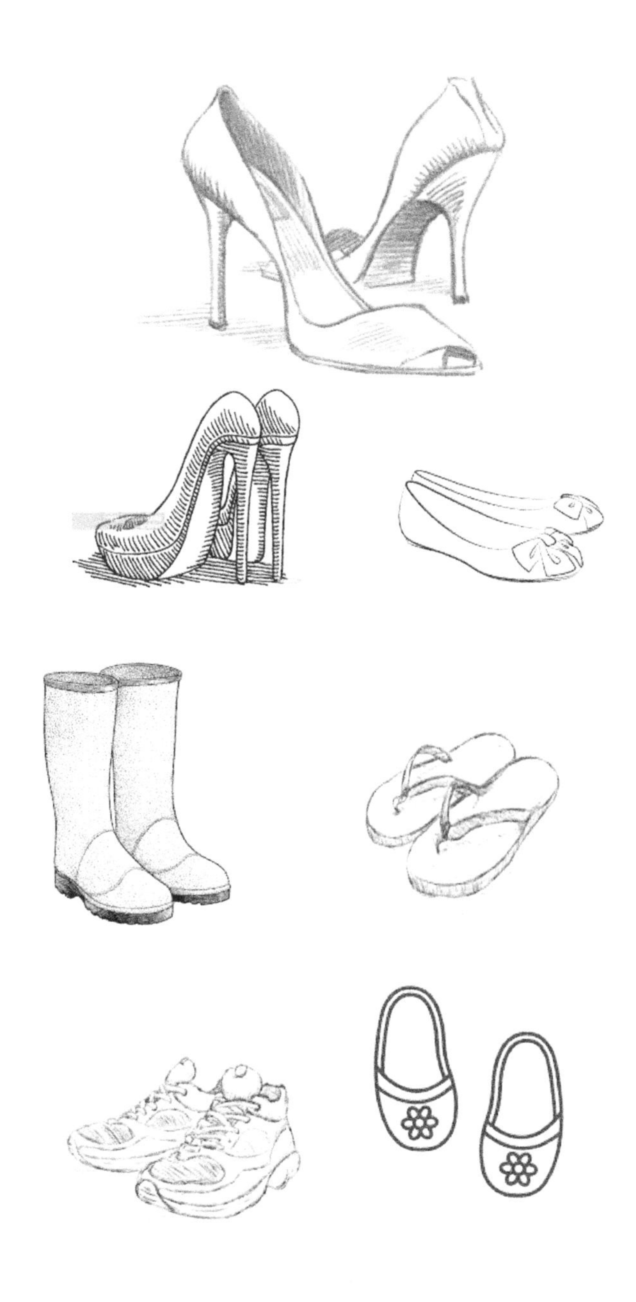

If you are struggling in life here is something to help you get back on track. I haven't always walk a straight path. The book *"Shoe Type Of Women"* help me see myself and I pray it does the same for you. God helped me get my life together. He broke me all the way down. Just pace yourself through the journal. Allow God to heal you completely. If you need to cry, scream, do it to beat whatever is holding you back from becoming a better person.

Father God I pray whoever pick this journal up that you touch them in a mighty way. God whatever is on they mind and in their heart I ask that you fix it God. God, we thank you for your healing power that is going to set many women free from bondage. We thank you for life again. Show each of us how to continue to walk in your Faithfulness, gentleness, love, and a peace of mind. You are truly worthy of it all in JESUS name AMEN.

THE ARMOR OF GOD

[10] Finally, be strong in the Lord and in his mighty power.

[11] Put on the full armor of God, so that you can take your stand against the devil's schemes.

[12] For our struggle is not against flesh and blood, but against the rulers, against the authorities, against the powers of this dark world and against the spiritual forces of evil in the heavenly realms.

[13] Therefore put on the full armor of God, so that when the day of evil comes, you may be able to stand your ground, and after you have done everything, to stand.

[14] Stand firm then, with the belt of truth buckled around your waist, with the breastplate of righteousness in place, [15] and with your feet fitted with the readiness that comes from the gospel of peace. [16] In addition to all this, take up the shield of faith, with which you can extinguish all the flaming arrows of the evil one. [17] Take the helmet of salvation and the sword of the Spirit, which is the word of God.

[18] And pray in the Spirit on all occasions with all kinds of prayers and requests. With this in mind, be alert and always keep on praying for all the Lord's people.

[19] Pray also for me, that whenever I speak, words may be given me so that I will fearlessly make known the mystery of the gospel, [20] for which I am an ambassador in chains. Pray that I may declare it fearlessly, as I should.

Wrong Shoes

Warnings come before destruction.

PROVERBS 16:18
NEW KING JAMES VERSION

18 Pride *goes* before destruction,
And a haughty spirit before [a]a fall.

Date: ____/____/____

What are somethings that you have done wrong that you want to change and do what's right?

Date: ____/____/____

Date: ____/____/____

Date: ____/____/____

Date: ____/____/____

Date: ____/____/____

Date: ____/____/____

Date: ____/____/____

Date: ____/____/____

Date: ____/____/____

Date: ____/____/____

Date: ____/____/____

TIGHT SHOES

True contentment comes from surrendering yourself to the only one who can satisfy your needs. Which is Christ JESUS!

Isaiah 45:22

International Standard Version

Turn to Me and be saved, all the ends of the earth;

For I am God, and there is no other.

Date: ____/____/____

Tight situations can lead you into dangerous places. To where you can't get out of. Pray and write some things to help you

Turn

Into

God's

Heart

&

TRUST

HIS WILL...

Date: ____/____/____

Date: ____/____/____

Date: ____/____/____

Date: ____/____/____

Date: ____/____/____

Date: ____/____/____

Date: ____/____/____

Date: ____/____/____

Date: ____/____/____

Date: ____/____/____

Date: ____/____/____

Date: ____/____/____

HURTING SHOE

Help Understand Release Transform

Psalm 34:18
New International Version

[18] The LORD is close to the brokenhearted
and saves those who are crushed in spirit.

Date: ____/____/____

***H**elp yourself **U**nderstand the pain so that you can **R**elease it out to*

*be able to **T**ransform into a healing person!*

Start off by saying what is hurting you........

In order to get **HELP** you must be able to write it out. God already knows what it is and wants to **HELP** you.

Understand what happen. Sometimes we do not want to face the pain. So, we become sad, and depressed. I have been there. Understand that if someone done something to you it is not your fault. Write a Pray and just talk to God the only one who understand our hearts.

RELEASE IT!! Tell your Story

Transform (Let's walk in our healing) How will you be able to tell someone your testimony

Date: ____/____/____

Date: ____/____/____

Date: ____/____/____

Date: ____/____/____

Date: ____/____/____

Date: ____/____/____

Date: ____/____/____

Date: ____/____/____

Date: ____/____/____

Date: ____/____/____

Date: ____/____/____

Date: ____/____/____

Date: ____/____/____

Date: ____/____/____

Date: ____/____/____

Date: ____/____/____

Date: ____/____/____

Date: ____/____/____

RUNNING SHOE

Stop running from your past issues...

Galatians 5:7
New International Version

[7] You were running a good race. Who cut in on you to keep you from obeying the truth?

Date: ____/____/____

Let's slow down and talk about Why are you running so much...

Date: ____/____/____

Date: ____/____/____

Date: ____/____/____

Date: ____/____/____

Date: ____/____/____

Date: ____/____/____

Date: ____/____/____

Date: ____/____/____

Date: ____/____/____

Date: ____/____/____

Date: ____/____/____

Date: ____/____/____

Flip Flop Shoe

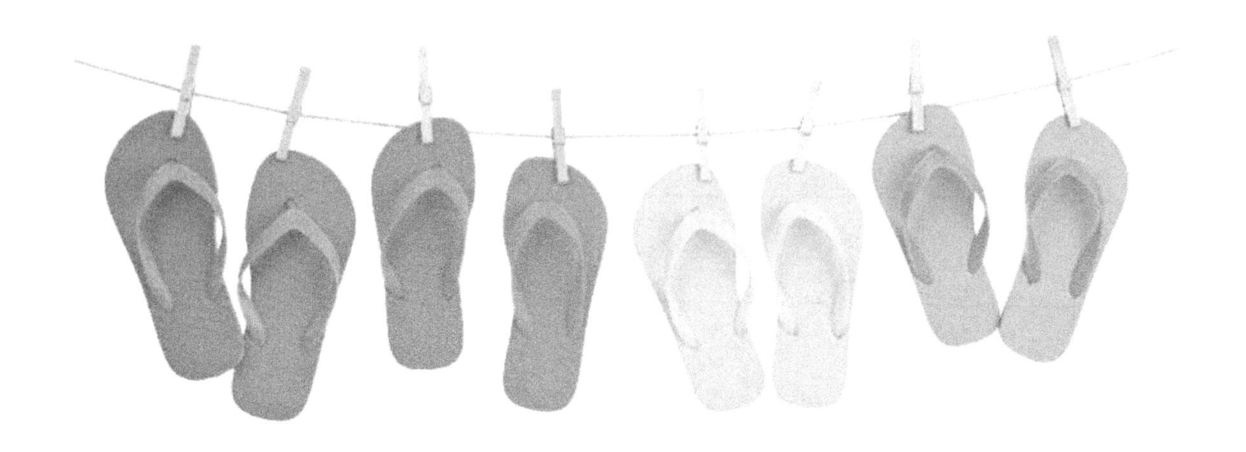

Watch how you flip flopping around in other people lives.

Psalm 34:13
New International Version

[13] keep your tongue from evil
and your lips from telling lies.

Date: ____/____/____

Date: ____/____/____

Date: ____/____/____

Date: ____/____/____

Date: ____/____/____

Date: ____/____/____

Date: ____/____/____

Date: ____/____/____

Date: ____/____/____

Date: ____/____/____

Date: ____/____/____

Date: ____/____/____

Date: ____/____/____

Date: ____/____/____

Date: ____/____/____

Flat Shoe

Are you dying of Oxygen?

Date: ____/____/____

Do not give up until you

***F**ind...*

***L**ife...*

***A**fter...*

***T**reatment...*

Seek the LORD for deliverance!

Date: ____/____/____

Date: ____/____/____

Date: ____/____/____

Date: ____/____/____

Date: ____/____/____

Date: ____/____/____

Date: ____/____/____

Date: ____/____/____

Date: ____/____/____

Date: ____/____/____

Date: ____/____/____

Right Shoe

Walk into Righteousness

2 Corinthians 5:7
New International Version

[7] For we live by faith, not by sight.

Date: ____/____/____

Starting Life, the right way can be hard, but give it a try with God on your side. He is able to do anything but fail. It is a process. Write a pray for the next 10 days and watch how things begin to change in your life.

Date: ____/____/____

Date: ____/____/____

Date: ____/____/____

Date: ____/____/____

Date: ____/____/____

Date: ____/____/____

Date: ____/____/____

Date: ____/____/____

Date: ____/____/____

Date: ____/____/____

Date: ____/____/____

Date: ____/____/____

Made in the USA
Middletown, DE
07 October 2022